MONSTER
MAX
AND THE BOBBLE HAT OF FORGETTING

MONSTER MAX
AND THE BOBBLE HAT OF FORGETTING

ROBIN BENNETT

ILLUSTRATED BY
TOM TINN-DISBURY

Firefly

First published in 2021
by Firefly Press
25 Gabalfa Road, Llandaff North, Cardiff, CF14 2JJ
www.fireflypress.co.uk

A CIP catalogue record of this book is available from the
British Library.

1 3 5 7 9 8 6 4 2

ISBN 9781913102333
ebook ISBN 9781913102340

*This book has been published with the support of the Books
Council Wales.*

Typeset and designed by
Alex Dimond

Printed and bound by CPI Group (UK) ltd, Croydon, CR0 4YY

Dedication

For our three monsters:
Jude, Victor and Hortense
RB

For Toby, a Monster Max in the making
T T-D

1

MEET MAX

This is Max.

Everything normal here.
Nothing weird about Max.

Max lives with his parents, David and Sally Forbes, who own a normal terraced house, on an ordinary street in a quiet (and very respectable) town.

This is Max's cat, Frankenstein.

And here's another picture, taken of Max and Frankenstein just last week.

OK, so there's something going on here.

You see, Max is sometimes a boy, who does all the boy things: like go to school, occasionally remember to do his homework, pretend to brush his teeth … BUT sometimes he is a monster who does all the monster things: like jump out of unlikely places, roar loudly, eat whole dustbins.

When he is a monster, Max sometimes forgets that Frankenstein is his best friend and wonders instead what cat tastes like…

Horrible – luckily.

'You have to stop turning yourself into a big hairy monster,' said Max's dad, one morning at breakfast. 'There's a report in the paper. People are *saying* things.'

'I can't help it,' said Max pouring himself some cereal.

[*Important Note*: This is not completely true. Max is very special: he can turn himself into a monster whenever he wants – he just has to **BURP**. And he can turn himself back into a small, grubby boy again just by **SNEEZING**. He has taught himself how, but (as you will find out) sometimes he burps by mistake and Max is allergic to flowers, which make him sneeze, so when he turns back into a boy again, it is hardly ever the right moment.]

'Then you'll have to work something out,' his dad continued. 'It says here that last night something that may have been *a bloodcurdling monster:*

- scared several old ladies at bus stops all over Oxford
- and climbed a tall statue in the park and shouted 'Bum!'

Luckily, the paper says it was probably someone in a costume ... although a Mrs Mudford-Sock of Mamble Drive is sure it was next door's poodle. But you can't keep becoming a monster and scaring people.'

'I read a book, too.'

'Well, reading books is good,' Max's dad admitted. 'Well done.'

'See? You should look on the bright side more often, Dad,' said Max.

'Hmm. Anyway,' said his dad, 'you need an M.O....'

'Half a *Moo*? Like if your cow's in a hurry?'

'No: a modus operandi. It's a purpose. Whenever you turn into a monster you think of something good to do...' Max's dad held up a picture in the paper. It showed a picture of the local chip van upside down in a duck pond. 'Instead of this.'

'I think that was Frankenstein...'

'No, it wasn't,' said Max's dad.

That evening, while he was watching TV, Max *did* think about things. It was fun turning himself into a Hairy Beast. He could run like the wind, he was super strong, he could climb up buildings and eat anything … except Frankenstein. Best of all, no one could tell him what to do.

He went to the kitchen via the hidden staircase in his room and picked up the newspaper that was lying on the table. Broken lampposts, smashed windows, metal statues of important people bent to look like they were picking their nose…

It was strange. Max couldn't remember doing any of it, but he was the only invincible monster in his town, so it must have been him, surely?

His dad was right, he needed to be more responsible. Besides anything else, he did not want to get his parents into trouble. Max was smart enough to know that being different made stuff harder sometimes.

He would go out tonight, he decided, and try not to break anything or gobble anyone up. Perhaps he might get an idea for an M.O....

MIDNIGHT MONSTERING

A full moon floated up into the night sky like a giant silver balloon, shining down on the quiet streets and houses with their neat front gardens and cosy chimneys. Max could see everything as if it were daytime.

Perfect monstering conditions.

Max didn't like to admit it but, even when he was a monster, he was still a bit scared of the dark.

Frankenstein, napping at the end

of Max's bed, woke up and looked at him hopefully. Frankenstein enjoyed monstering almost as much as Max did.

Max checked it was all clear: both his parents were safely tucked up in bed, fast asleep, and the street outside was dead quiet.

He crept down to the kitchen and made a monster sandwich with roast ham, hot pickles, cheese, ketchup, a handful of salty crisps, and chocolate sprinkles for good measure. He looked at it for a few moments, then gobbled it up.

Then he burped giantly and felt his PJs ripping as he grew muscles, hair and big teeth.

19

One of the best things about being a monster is you don't need to use the stairs. But he'd promised his mum he'd stop smashing windows, so Max had built a special Monster Door.

Unfortunately, he forgot about Dad's greenhouse.

Oops, thought Max, not a good start. He sniffed the cool night air with his monster nose. Right, now what?

Max looked about for a bit, roared at the moon and climbed a tall tree. Streetlights shone on quiet terraced houses with their sloping roofs, on Mr Nadeem's shop that sold everything and on St Anthony's church advertising a coffee morning for the over 60s. The only sign of life came from Dave's Kebab n' Chip van in the lay-by near the park.

Max decided to go somewhere he wasn't going to cause any trouble: the local rubbish dump. Everything was already broken there and they had great puddles.

Frankenstein loved the rubbish dump, too.

After making the most of the puddles, Max built a futuristic house out of old washing machines for the people who worked at the dump to shelter in when it rained. Then he felt hungry, so he ate an old lawnmower. He was just licking his monster lips, wondering what else to do, when he heard a curious knocking sound.

He turned to see the pointy top of a bright red hat poking out from a pile of old tyres. The owner of the hat was banging on something.

'Gna gna gna gna gna,' it said, in a way that made Max's monster hair stand up. The tyre tower wobbled.

Max was about to go and investigate when he heard another, more familiar sound: a car engine. It came from the locked gates at the other end of the yard.

Forgetting the pointy hat and the banging, Max peered around the corner and saw a big man climb out of a rusty van. He had badly drawn tattoos on his neck and he was carrying a large pair of cutters.

Max watched as the man snapped the lock with his cutters and kicked the gates open with his giant, muddy boots.

'Sorted!' the large man shouted at the other person driving the van. 'Hurry up, Spike, we 'aven't got all night.'

Max's monster hair really bristled now, something that always happened when danger was about. He watched carefully as the van drove into the dump and parked.

Spike got out of the driver's seat. He was very boney with tufts of hair on his head and chin, which made him look like a cross camel, and he had a gold tooth that glinted in the moonlight. 'Well, Grinder,' he said in a raspy voice, 'that was easy.'

'Why are we 'ere, anyway?' Grinder asked, his big hand scratching his big bottom.

'We've got to open this safe with all that money from St Cuthbert's Primary School Charity Knicker Knitting Competition and they've got all the sledge hammers and drills for the job in the shed … and it's so far away from anywhere, no one will hear all the sawing and drilling.'

'Oh, right. I still feel bad stealing all that money from the kiddies,' said Grinder.

'Well, you won't be feeling so bad when you're having the holiday of a lifetime somewhere hot and sunny,' Spike snapped. 'Har, har!'

Grinder opened the van door and Max could see the huge black safe inside. There was also a bunch of roses. 'Let me find some water to put these in,' he said, picking up the roses.

'Don't know why you took them,' said Spike. 'We've got all their money from their Christmas collection. You can afford a hundred bunches of flowers.'

'They're for the wife, she likes flowers–'

Spike grabbed the roses from Grinder and threw them across the dump.

They landed by Max.

Uh oh, thought Max and sneezed…

Spike whipped around like a snake, his tooth glinting in the moonlight.

'What was that?' Grinder said.

'Dunno, but it came from there.' Spike pointed a long, dirty finger right where Max was hiding. 'If there's someone spying on us, they're going to wish they had stayed at home!'

Max looked down at himself, hoping he was still a monster, but the sneezing had done what it always did – he was back to being a boy. A boy who only had his pants on. And they were very loose.

Frankenstein gave a miaow that sounded more like a gulp and Max looked up to see Spike glaring down at him.

'What the–?' Spike's mouth hung open and Max saw lots of rotten teeth and a few gaps: Spike obviously hardly ever brushed his teeth. The gold one seemed to be holding all the others in place. 'It's a kid in his underpants,' he growled. 'Right, let's be having you.'

He reached down just as Frankenstein leapt at Spike and scratched his arm.

'Ow! Why you 'orrible mangy cat, when I get my hands on you…'

Max knew that this was his only chance. 'Thanks, Frankenstein,' he shouted, sprinting towards the gate, holding his pants up with one hand.

Spike and Grinder took a second to react but then they came lumbering after him. Spike grabbed the large bolt cutters.

Max was running as fast as he could, but he could tell the men were going to catch him in seconds. This is serious, thought Max. He wanted to burp but he was a bit busy running for his life: he didn't want to think what Spike would do with those cutters when he caught him.

He took a big gulp of air and tried to speed up. But the air went down the wrong way and instead...

He burped.

It was a huge burp: it rattled all the car windows in the dump and echoed off the tower of washing machines.

'Roar!' said Max the Monster, turning around to face two very surprised robbers. 'Roaaaaarrrrrrrr!!!!!!!!!!!!!!!'

'Run for your life,' said Spike, dropping the cutters on his giant, bony toe.

'I want my mummy,' whimpered Grinder.

Max chased Grinder and Spike for a very long time. All the way to the police station, in fact. Then he went back to the rubbish dump and picked up the safe with all the money in it.

It was very heavy, but Max carried it

back to St Cuthbert's Primary School without any trouble at all.

It was a shame he had to leave the flowers behind.

The next morning, Max was starving after all his monstering, so he had a giant fry-up breakfast. With extra bacon.

Max's dad sat across the kitchen table looking very pleased about something. He was smiling to himself and humming as he ate his toast, sending buttery breadcrumbs flying all over the newspaper he was reading.

Max looked at the front cover.

'Monster Fancy-Dress Hero Saves Charity Knicker Knitting Kitty Cash.'

There was also a picture of Grinder and Spike being led away by the police.

'It's a fair cop,' said the hardened criminal. 'Take me to your darkest, deepest prison, I don't mind, I deserve it. But just don't let that horrible scary monster near me. I'll never steal anything again.'

'Fancy-dress, indeed! Was that anything to do with you, Maxwell?' Max's mother had come back from her early morning line dancing class. She always called him Maxwell when she was being strict.

'Um,' Max thought about it. He didn't want to get into trouble, but he was getting a bit too old for telling fibs. 'It might have been.' He turned to his father. 'I think I've found my M.O., Dad.'

'Oh?'

'To protect and do good stuff!'

There was a long silence. Max looked at his dad, who winked back. Max's mum smiled the slow secret smile of a wolf and ruffled Max's hair.

'Well done, Max,' she whispered.

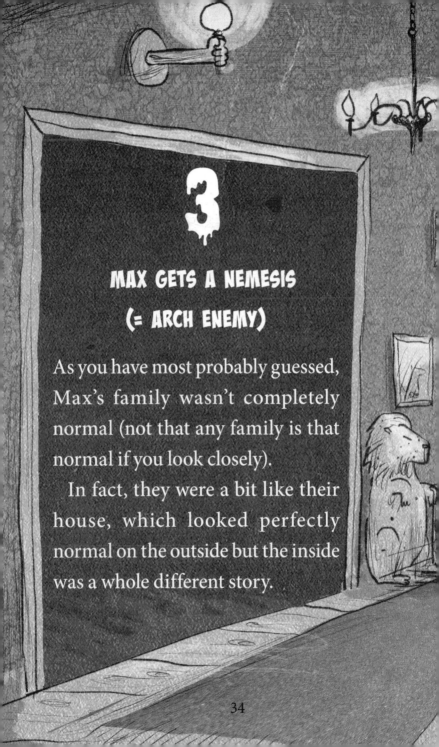

3

MAX GETS A NEMESIS
(= ARCH ENEMY)

As you have most probably guessed, Max's family wasn't completely normal (not that any family is that normal if you look closely).

In fact, they were a bit like their house, which looked perfectly normal on the outside but the inside was a whole different story.

Most of the time, Max's mum did Mum Things like take Max to school, help him with his homework and yell instructions up the stairs. However, where she was born in Krit, a tiny country between Transylvania and Moldova, being able to change into a monster, wolf, bear or bat wasn't considered unusual. In Krit, it was pretty strange if you couldn't turn yourself into some sort of creature.

Krit is the smallest country in the whole world. The whole of Krit fits on top of one tall, pointy mountain with clouds covering its middle, so most people, even those who live further down the mountain, don't even know it is there.

Krit, as a country, is amazing at fitting

Krit

a great deal into very little space and some of that magic had rubbed off on their previously normal terrace house that seemed to sprout extra rooms the way most of the other houses in their street sprouted neat rows of daffodils and petunias.

The next morning, they were in the

kitchen, eating toast. As usual.

'Dad, how did you meet Mum?'

'I've told you a squillion times.'

'I know, but I like hearing the story.'

Max's dad beamed, because he liked telling it.

'Well, your mother's country has always fascinated me.' His eyes twinkled. 'Because of all the secrets, the mystery and the magic … and interesting clouds.'

Max's dad liked clouds. A lot. He was a nephrologist, which is the name for a person who studies clouds.

'And so one day you packed a rucksack and just went there, because there's no point putting off for tomorrow what you can do today!' said Max.

'Quite right. So, there I was, with just about everything I owned on my back,

my hat and a compass. It was a long
climb up to Krit, as there is only one
path. It winds around and around the
mountain like a giant snake. When I
climbed past the clouds, I found myself
in a huge, dark forest.'

'Don't forget the bit about the wolves, Dad.'

'How could I? They chased me through the trees. Howling their heads off.'

'Were you scared?'

'I knew I had my secret weapon.'

'Squeaky toys!'

'Yes! Werewolves can't resist squeaky toys. So I tamed the biggest and fiercest with a rubber chicken that went quack, and they took me back to their secret village.'

'What was it like?' asked Max, although he knew the answer.

'It was amazing. It was coming up to full moon and most of the inhabitants had become their creature-selves: there were Rock Giants as tall as a house…'

'Sprites as small as a butterfly!' chorused Max.

'Yes! And the wolves! Beautiful animals, twice the size of a normal wolf and separated into packs by the colour of their eyes: the gentle greys, like your mother, the mysterious (and very rare) silvers and, finally, the brooding, dangerous wolves with flecks that burned red in deep wells of black. These last ones hunted deep in the forest, where no light can go, even on the sunniest day. The King of Krit – a gentle giant of a wolf called Vulpinx – introduced me to his daughter, princess Vulpina.'

'Mum?'

'Yup.'

'Did she try and gobble you up?'

'No, even when she was being a scary wolf, I could tell she fancied me.'

'Urgh, Dad!'

'When you're not there, we kiss on the lips.'

'DAD!!'

'Well, you asked.'

'No, I didn't,' said Max firmly. 'I just meant weren't you worried when you came back to England and everyone knew she was different because she came from Krit … and the secret turning-into-a-wolf thing?'

'Well,' said his dad, 'different is good, don't ever forget that. And we're polite to people and we always help out at the jumble sale, so people we know like us. But you're right, we keep your monster thing and her wolf thing a secret. Some people wouldn't understand. Krit is the only place in the world with all this magic and it's safer if other people don't know.'

Max thought about it. 'How did you get Mum to come to England? Did you give her a squeaky chicken too?'

'Not exactly.'

'I just like to try new things!' said his mum, coming into the kitchen with an armful of plastic bags from Mr Nadeem's Food Emporium. She always did the shopping after her unicycling class.

'But there was some trouble with a huge Red Eye called Fanghorn.' Max's dad went back to the story. 'He was going to be chief after Vulpinx and marry your mother. He's chief of the pack now. He didn't like me and even to this day he wants your mother back.'

'Surely Fanghorn must have calmed down by now?' Max asked.

'I don't think so,' said Mum darkly. 'We only were able to leave because your father managed to trick him into putting on the Bobble Hat of Forgetting.'

'The what of Forgetting?' This was new.

'The Bobble Hat of Forgetting,' said his mother, with the completely straight face she only used when she was trying not to smile. 'It was knitted by witches who live in the ice caves at the very top of the mountain. It's very cold up there, as you can imagine, so bobble hats are very popular presents any time of year – but the witches infused it with a charm of befuddlement.'

'Befuddly-what?'

'It means anyone who wears it will become confused and forget what they were doing. Fanghorn only wore it for a minute or two, but that was enough time for us to get away without him seeing where we went.'

'It was one of the only things we bought from Krit,' added his father.

'But wolves from their clan never really forget and you can be sure they are still keeping an eye out for us.'

'Fanghorn is my nemesis!' exclaimed Max's dad proudly.

'What's a nemesis?'

'It's an arch enemy.'

Just then there was a ring on the doorbell.

'I'll get it!' Max loved answering the door.

'Hello,' said a boy standing on the doorstep. The boy, who was about Max's age, wore his school uniform, even though it was a Saturday morning, and had his hair parted down the side, like the sort of grown up who talks about roads, safety instructions and other boring things. Max didn't like him immediately.

'Can I help you?' asked Max in a way that really meant, I hope you go away.

'Well, that remains to be seen, whoever you are. My name is Peregrine and I am a seeker of the truth and a genius inventor!'

'What do you want?' asked Max, unimpressed.

'I'm looking into the irresponsible activities of a horrible creature seen recently in our neighbourhood. It has been smashing things, scaring people and generally being a nuisance. Some say it's someone in disguise, others think it's a poodle – but you can't fool Peregrine: it's a dangerous monster who should be captured and locked up in a laboratory for experiments.'

'If you mean the amazing, incredibly brave, very helpful, stupendously good-looking and intelligent monster that has been helping out in the community by catching criminals...' Max paused. He didn't like the look of keen interest on the boy's face one bit. 'Then I've got no idea what you are talking about. Goodbye!'

He went to slam the door, but the annoying boy had stuck his foot in the way.

'Not so fast, young man.'

'We're the same age. Move your foot, nerdy face.'

'In years we are the same, perhaps, but I am your intellectual superior.'

'You look like you've got an egg whisk on your head, with your grandpa's glasses glued to it,' said Max, who had no idea what an Intellectual Superior was, but had just decided he really, really did not like this boy, who was now trying to shove past him into the house.

As he pushed the door with his shoulder, the boy was clipping the strange machine to the top of his head. Then he pulled out a spiky antennae and a pair of goggles and attached it. He glared at Max down his long nose.

'This,' he said, 'is my Personal Animal Nano Tracking Sonar – P. A. N. T. S. for short.'

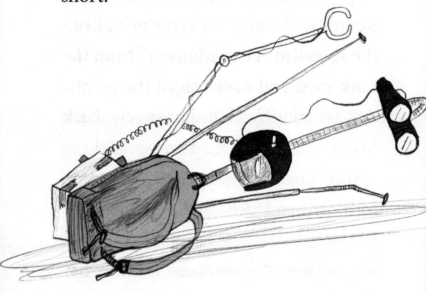

'Seriously, pants?' said Max, grinning, even as he tried with all his strength to shut the door. 'You may want to think about calling it something else.'

'So childish,' said the boy. 'Not that you could possibly understand with your tiny brain, but this device is designed to track the footsteps – or claw steps – of any living creature. I took a sample in the mud off a paw print from the so-called "Hero Monster" from the junk yard and have traced the prints, that are invisible to the human eye, back to this house. I want answers!'

Max shouted the first thing that came into his head. 'Look, Yeti! Help, save me from this Abominable Snowman!' He pointed somewhere behind his unwelcome visitor.

'What, where?!' Peregrine turned around, grappling with his P.A.N.T.S.. Most importantly, he took his foot out of the door.

'Ha! Obviously Peregrine can be fooled – and pretty easily at that!' cried

Max, slamming the door firmly shut. 'Not so smart after all!'

There was a pause.

'I'll be back,' said the muffled voice of Peregrine through the door. 'I don't give up that easily. Especially when there is a dangerous wild animal on the loose that should be locked away!'

'Who was that?' asked his dad, as Max came back into the kitchen.

Max didn't say anything for a moment. He was thinking about the boy and remembering what his dad had said about enemies.

'Well…?'

'He's called Peregrine. He's my nemesis.'

A CRAFTY PLAN

For a whole week, each time Max looked out of the window, Peregrine was there with his stupid P.A.N.T.S. machine. Even at night.

I've got to do something, thought Max. Ever since Peregrine had knocked on their door, Max had not been able to carry out any of his new hero-ing duties. He hadn't even dared turn into a monster. Not once.

It was boring.

He looked out of the window, thinking about this boy waiting to capture a monster (Max) and about the red-eyed wolf, Fanghorn, waiting all these years to get his revenge.

Max realised the problem wasn't only him being a monster. What if Peregrine found out his mum was a wolf? He might capture her too and send her back to Krit ... and Fanghorn!

Max made up his mind: the Peregrine Problem needed to be sorted out.

He stared out of the window some more.

Soon a crafty plan formed in his head.

That night he sneaked out through the secret tunnel behind the fireplace in the ballroom. Max had been hard at work all afternoon cutting up an old broom, a pair of his mother's washing-up gloves and bits of wire he'd found in the remains of the garden shed.

Madame Pinky-Ponky helped him with the gluing and fiddly bits. She was an old family friend who had travelled to England with his mother from Krit and she was very good at making things – especially breakfasts, very large sandwiches and cakes (all of which was fine by Max). Madame Pinky-Ponky had silvery hair, like dandelion silk, and loved Max like a granny. That afternoon she showed him how to stuff the rubber gloves with tissue paper and stick them to the two halves of the broom handle.

Soon everything was ready. He used the wire to make realistic claws.

'Well done, Max!' Madame PP beamed at him. 'Although I've no idea why you need to make a pair of monster feet – you've got your own!'

'It's a secret,' said Max.

He went off and found some red paint that was lying about.

Now he was in the secret passageway leading from the ballroom out into a back street behind Honeybrooke Road. There were quite a few of these tunnels in their cellar, leading to all sorts of interesting places, but no one except Max used them because they were dusty and it was easy to get lost.

Heh heh, thought Max, standing in the short alleyway that ran past their house. He dipped the fake monster feet into the red paint and started making gloopy red paw prints all the way down the pavement, past the end of the road where the eternally annoying Peregrine was staking out their house. 'This will keep him busy.'

Max had been watching Peregrine almost as much as Peregrine had been spying on the house and Max knew he would spot the prints sooner or later, when he did his rounds.

Max carried on making paw prints across two more roads, past the bus stop, then through a small park. The paint was running out

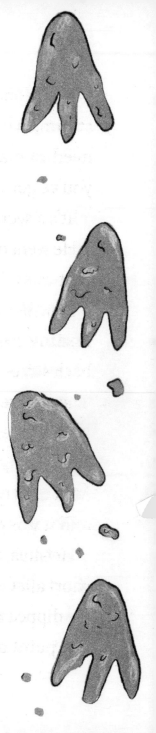

now, so Max looked around for ideas.

'Ah ha!' he said out loud, his eyes narrowing. Just in front of him was a manhole cover. It was big and rusty and Max would never be able to move it on his own. He made sure no one was watching, then he burped.

Monster Max lifted the heavy cover as if it was as light as a paper plate.

Inside the sewer, the smell was terrible, even for a monster: hundred-year-old poo and wee. The walls were brown and the water below made gluggy, farty noises as it gurgled along.

Max stared about. His monster eyes could see perfectly in the dark. Curiously, he could tell he wasn't the only one to be down here recently: small footprints ran through the mud at the edge of the tunnel. They didn't look like rats' or mice's; they almost looked human, except tiny. Seeing them gave Max a funny feeling, as if he should know what they were but couldn't remember, like a feeling in a dream.

He shrugged off the strange thoughts – he had a job to do!

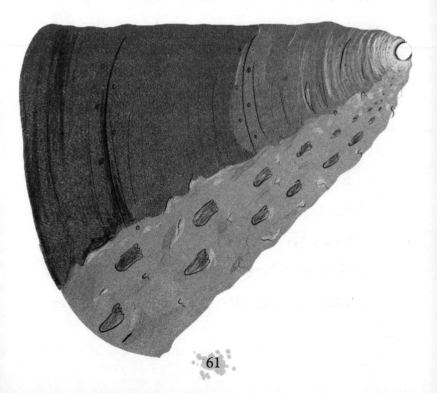

Max made more fake Monster prints all the way down the steps, into this stinky, dark and gurgling place. When the pot of paint was finished, he threw the broom handles away.

'Grat was gruky,' he said. It was hard to talk through giant monster teeth.

As he climbed out, he was careful to leave the manhole cover open just enough so Peregrine could get down without having to lift it up.

Now, he needed to change back to Max. He looked about and saw a rose bush in someone's front garden…

TO PROTECT AND DO GOOD STUFF!

Max's plan had worked better than he could have expected. He had raced up the secret staircase and into his bedroom, just in time to see Peregrine disappear around the house on one of his hourly patrols.

Max waited. Peregrine did not come back. For a very long time.

He's been fooled, thought Max gleefully, picturing his enemy paddling through the yukky brown water, trying to track down where the big red footprints had disappeared to. He almost felt a bit sorry for Peregrine, but remembered that this was the boy who wanted to get Max (and probably his mum) locked up.

Anyway, there were plenty of ways out, so Peregrine was unlikely to be lost for long – just long enough, Max hoped, to put him off monster-chasing for good.

The very next night, Max gave Frankenstein his supper. 'Right,' he said to his cat, who was looking at him expectantly, 'time to protect and do good stuff!' He took out a can of fizzy orange from the fridge and drank it in one gulp.

Max gave a huge burp, startling the cat, and sprang out of his bedroom window, into a large bush.

He wasn't taking any chances, so Max sent Frankenstein first, to check the coast was clear, then stepped out of the bush and into the quiet night.

His first good deed was to move a fallen tree that was blocking the cycle path and plant it back in the ground. Then he gobbled up a load of rubbish someone had tipped on the side of the road instead of taking it to the town recycling unit. The old armchair, in particular, was nice and chewy.

Max climbed to the top of the statue opposite the town hall and had a good look about. It was very quiet. Frankenstein got bored and went hunting for old fish heads in the park bins.

Max loved being a monster. As long as it wasn't too cloudy (and dark), he loved being out at night: the light, the sounds, even the smells were different. It may have seemed quiet, but there was plenty going on, if you had super-powerful eyesight.

Far over, right over the other side of town, he could see an owl sitting on the ledge of a church tower. He heard a rustle and looked down: just under the trees a family of mice were getting up to go out for the night. Much further away, he heard a boat moving quietly through the still waters of the Thames. Max sniffed the air and smelled damp grass, the delicious sizzling aroma of meat from the Kebab van, then smoke…

Hang on… He sniffed the air again.

If he'd been a normal boy, he may not have noticed anything (and he wouldn't have been perched on top of Queen Victoria's head in the first place) but with his improved monster eyesight, he spotted a smudge of smoke drifting across the sky in the distance.

Fire!

In a single leap, he jumped from the statue onto a nearby roof. Frankenstein saw him and caught up. The two raced along the rooftops faster than any car could go by road.

As they got closer to the smoke, Monster Max saw the orange-and-red glow of flames against the darkness and his monster ears heard someone cry out. Max put on extra speed, leaping from roof to roof in a blur of fur. He skidded to a halt on the tiles of a small house in a quiet close.

Smoke ran up the front wall of the house as two frightened faces looked out of a bedroom window at the fire on the ground floor.

Max jumped through the black smoke

and caught hold of the roof ledge just above their room. The fire made the tiles hot but Max's monster feet were covered in thick monster skin that didn't feel a thing.

Gripping the tiles with his long claws, he swung upside down over the window where the children were trapped.

'Rero there!' said Max, in his friendliest voice, and pointed at the window latch. 'Ropennup, prease.'

The elder, a girl about two years younger than Max, backed away – not surprising given a monster had just appeared outside their bedroom. The younger girl, who was only about three, turned and looked at the angry orange flames flicking under the door to their bedroom. She started to cry.

'Rookout!' said Max, pointing at the
black smoke gathering around their
bare feet. But his big sharp claws were
making the small girls even more scared
of him than the fire.

The flames were angry red now and Max could feel the heat through the window. He thought about smashing it, but flying glass might cut the children. He listened for the sound of a fire engine and heard it very faintly, very far away. It would arrive too late. It was all up to him.

Smoke started to drift along the gutter. Max's nose felt tickly and he had an idea: it was risky but it was his only option. He climbed onto the narrow window ledge, taking a second to get his balance. Then he breathed in.

And sneezed.

The girls stared as the scary monster at their window changed into a boy not much older than them. He was struggling not to fall.

'Open the window!' he shouted.

'It's locked!' the elder girl shouted back. 'I don't know where my parents put the key. They went out for pizza.'

'Help, I'm scared!' the little girl cried.

'Cover your face with a teddy,' shouted Max through the window, fighting to keep his balance on the narrow ledge. 'It will stop you breathing in the smoke.' He turned to the elder girl. 'You do the same with a pillow. Stand back from the window and turn your head. I'm going to break it.'

The fire was very hot now. Max didn't have any more time.

'I'm going to have to be scary again, but I'm not going to hurt you. Do you believe me?'

The little girl looked at Max with large

round eyes and slowly nodded.

Max took a huge gulp of air and burped.

With one punch, he broke the window and gathered up the children in his long monster arms, trying not to drop them or squeeze them too hard. He jumped to the ground. He did a somersault for added showing off.

Max turned to the house. The flames filled the living room.

'ROAR!' roared Max in his roariest voice.

All the windows of the house smashed. The flames blew out immediately and all the smoke disappeared up the chimney.

At that moment, the children's parents appeared in their car, with cries of alarm and relief to see their girls safe and sound. Pizza boxes flew in the air as the children were gathered up and hugged.

Luckily, it was very dark. Otherwise the mum and dad would have seen a big hairy monster standing on their front lawn, even if he was trying to hide behind a bush, and Max was pretty sure they would have something to say about that.

The fire brigade arrived and took charge.

Time to go, he thought. He was just getting ready to jump onto the roof when something small but very fast shot out of some bins and knocked Monster Max off his feet. Max glimpsed the very same pointy red hat he'd seen at the dump and heard the buzz of very fast feet, followed by a bang as the thing went through the hedge at the end of the garden into a shed. Max's monster ears heard pots being smashed and giggling. 'Gna gna gna gna gna…'

Max realised he was lying on his back on the front lawn, small, muddy footprints running up his chest. Any second now, someone was going to turn around and see him and then he was going to have a lot of explaining to do.

Monster Max looked and saw the little girl he'd rescued staring at him over her mother's shoulder.

'Look,' she cried, pointing away from Max and back at the house. 'There's still a bit of fire on the roof!'

All grown-up eyes looked up at the chimney, instead of down at Monster

Max. It gave him enough time to escape.

Just before he yomped away into the night, he took one last look at the house. The little girl smiled and gave him a secret wave.

PEREGRINE RETURNS

The next morning Max got up a bit later than usual. It had been a busy night: his hair still smelled smoky. His mum was waiting for him on the stairs.

'Max? There are reports that a strange creature saved some children from a burning house. Was that anything to do with you?'

'Um, maybe…' said Max. He couldn't work out if his mum was cross or not.

'Hmm, well, luckily no one believed

the youngest when she said something hairy with long claws and pointy teeth got them out of the house, then put the fire out by shouting. They're saying there must have been a freak thunderstorm that put the fire out, just over their house, then blew all the smoke away.'

She looked at Max for a few seconds, as if still making up her mind about something, then gave him a big hug. Max normally wouldn't like hugs, but this morning it felt OK.

'Well done,' she said, 'I'm very proud of you … but I'm also very cross,' she added. 'Monster or not, you could have been hurt – any fire is very dangerous. I want you to promise me, Max, you won't do anything dangerous.'

Max nodded in a way he hoped looked

convincing and, to change the subject, told his mother about the thing in the red hat.

She listened carefully and pursed her lips – something she always did when she was worried but trying not to show it.

'Do you know what it is?' asked Max.

'I'm not sure,' she said. 'But I do know that it's all the more reason to be extra especially careful.'

'OK, Mum,' said Max grinning. 'Monster's Honour.'

'Yes, well, anyway, I asked Madam Pinky-Ponky to make you this, she's much better at sewing than me.' She held up something made of black velvet. It had a brass chain and looked like a cape that a superhero might wear. 'Look, it's even got a pocket for a hanky.'

'Really, Mum?'

'Very really. Even monsters need to blow their noses.'

'What's it actually for?'

'Well, first of all, whilst you are … um…'

'Protecting and doing good stuff!'

'Quite so. Well, you might need it to, um, cover yourself up, if you change back into just Max.'

Max thought about being chased by Grinder wearing just his pants. 'Good point.'

'Secondly, it's black, which will help you hide if you need to.'

'Thanks, Mum,' said Max, deciding a cape was actually just the thing he needed.

Just then the doorbell rang, followed by a loud banging at the door.

'That doesn't sound good,' said his dad, coming out of the bedroom with a large book about bagpipes. 'Do you want me to deal with it?'

'No, thank you,' said Max. 'I've got a feeling I know who it is.'

'I suppose you think that was funny?'

Peregrine, aged 10, Inventor and Monster Catcher, stood on the doorstep covered in slime and bits of toilet paper. He was holding the two fake monster feet and an empty pot of red paint.

'I don't know what you're talking about?' said Max, trying very hard not to laugh.

'Then how come the footprints led from the side of your house?'

Oops, thought Max.

Peregrine leaned in close. He smelled a bit pooey.

'You're hiding something and I think it's this monster. My drones show me it smashed all the windows in the burning house last night. It probably started the fire, too. And there's those other things it's been smashing all over town.'

Peregrine held up pictures of squashed bicycles, trees with no branches and a burst water main, all of which Max had never seen before.

'Actually, he saved those children from the fire and as for that other stuff ... he's a hero!' Max was too angry to make a proper sentence.

'Hmm, public menace, more like. What gives him the right to run about the place, breaking things and pretending to be brave? That's what we have the fire brigade for. They're trained! Anyway, I will find out where you are hiding it. I am declaring war on you, Max!'

'I'd go and have a shower first!' said Max, slamming the front door.

7

MAX GETS INTO TROUBLE

The very next day, a note came through the door.

Hand your monster over to the police immediately! If you do not do so by midnight tomorrow, I will come around to your house and capture it myself, using my newly invented and completely amazing device, the Portable Operating Omni Prison.

That spells Poop, thought Max with a smirk. Then he noticed there was some writing on the other side of the page.

P.S. I'm perfectly aware that spells Poop, and I don't care – you are such a baby.

Max, who had no intention of handing himself into a police station, was furious that Peregrine was blaming Max for all the smashed things he hadn't done.

Who would have been able to save those children from the fire except him?

Max needed to do something to stop Peregrine once and for all. He still had one advantage: Peregrine hadn't worked out yet that it was actually Max who was the monster (sometimes). He probably thought they were keeping a beast in a cage in the cellar or something, and they only let it out at night.

Just at that moment, Madame Pinky-Ponky tottered past with the tea tray, giving him another brilliant idea.

OK, I'm going to give him a night to remember, thought Max.

That evening, Max borrowed Madame Pinky-Ponky's long red scarf and her outdoors hat. Calling it a hat was stretching the point: it was really more a sort of big black umbrella you could wear on your head. Madame Pinky-Ponky hated to get wet and, on the rare occasions she set foot outside the house, she made sure she was triple protected against the British weather. Max didn't trust himself to walk in high heels, so he found some pink wellies and an old black coat in the boot room, and grabbed another umbrella while he was at it.

Max looked in the mirror. With the hat stuck on firmly over his ears and the scarf pulled up past his nose, he looked like any little old lady you might see walking about town. The coat smelled dusty and sort of elderly, which just added to the effect.

'Max?'

'Oh, hi, Dad.'

'Do we need to have a little chat about wearing lady's clothing?'

'What? Oh, this,' said Max. 'I'm going undercover.'

'So you're planning to infiltrate the Old Folks Sewing Bee and steal their recipes for fruit cake and jam roly-poly?'

'Sometimes you're quite funny, Dad,' said Max, opening the front door. 'Not today, though.'

'Whatever you are up to, be careful,' said Max's dad, his usually smiley face serious. But Max had already gone.

It didn't take Max long to find Peregrine: the P.O.O.P. machine stuck out over the hedge he was hiding in.

'Young man!' said Max, in his best old lady's voice. He gave the hedge a good shake with the umbrella.

'What?' said Peregrine a bit rudely. 'Go away, I'm busy.'

'Don't you "what" me, young man,' said Max, getting rather annoyed, 'and you're not busy, I've been watching you, you're just sitting there…'

'Shhh, I'm on a secret mission.'

'And don't you shush me, either. I can see that stupid thing on your head from across the street and I'm ninety-two and it's dark. Anyway, would your secret mission have anything to do with the big, hairy but curiously good-looking monster I've just seen, by any chance?'

'Yes, but I wouldn't say it was good-loo–'

'Well, you better hurry. It's up to all sorts.'

'Like what?' Peregrine came out from behind the hedge. Max's scarf slipped a bit, but luckily Peregrine was too busy looking down the road.

'Um…' Max tightened the scarf and tried to think of something quickly. 'It's crossing the road without looking.'

Peregrine looked a bit disappointed. 'Is that all?'

'Oh, um … no, that's just the start. It's on its way to the kennels. It's going to gobble up all the puppies. Quick! You have to save them.'

'Right!' exclaimed Peregrine, cocking

the crossbow that was attached to the P.O.O.P. machine.

'Hang about.' He stopped and looked suspiciously at Max, who wondered if his disguise was good enough. 'How do you know what it wants to do?'

'I'm a very good guesser! Now hurry up!' Max prodded Peregrine in the ribs with his umbrella.

'Ow! OK, keep your wig on,' said Peregrine. He started to jog down the road. Max overtook him easily.

'It's this way!' he shouted over his shoulder.

'You're very fast for an old, um … more mature lady.' Peregrine was struggling to keep up.

'I eat six chocolate bars every day for breakfast.'

'Isn't that bad for you?' asked Peregrine.

'Nonsense! Don't believe everything grown-ups tell you; they just want to keep all the good stuff for themselves. Here we are!' Max the old lady skidded to a halt in Madame Pinky-Ponky's pink wellies. 'This is where I last saw it. You go first, you're much braver than me.'

They were standing next to a small playground with a couple of swings, a climbing frame for very small children and a see-saw.

'In there?' Peregrine raised his crossbow. 'I can use the scope on the bow. It's infrared, so it can see in the dark and there's heat sensors on the side that will pick up anything living within five hundred metres. Which direction did you say it went?'

'I reckon it'll be just behind those trees by now. If you climb on top of the see-saw at one end, I'll sit on the other and it will lift you up. You'll be able to use that contraption of yours better.'

'Er, OK.' Peregrine didn't seem so sure.

'Hurry up, it's getting away! Stone the crows, it'll be tucking into half a dozen poodles before you do anything at this rate.'

Max watched carefully as Peregrine stood on the lowest seat. He's taken the bait, he thought, and gave a quiet burp…

Peregrine was looking the other way, over the tops of some trees, for a monster that was now sitting on the other end of the seesaw. Monster Max leapt up high and stomped down as hard as he could onto the see-saw's plastic seat. The other seat shot up and, with a yelp of surprise, so did Peregrine.

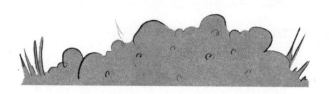

Monster Max watched with great satisfaction as Peregrine and his P.O.O.P. machine soared into the cold night air, heading towards the river Thames.

He waited for the sound of a splash, chuckling to himself in a monstery way. 'Gre heh heh!' He had a feeling he wouldn't be hearing from Peregrine for a while.

But Max was too busy giggling to notice a giant rubber sucker shoot out from the darkness. It stuck itself to the back of his shaggy head.

'GrOwch!' It was Monster Max's turn to be unpleasantly surprised. He tried to pull the sucker off but it had some kind of glue on the end.

On the non-sucker end was a long length of elastic rope. It now pulled tight. His monster ears picked up a whistling sound and Max turned just in time to see Peregrine returning to Earth very fast.

Crickey, thought Max.

Peregrine was coming down so fast, it looked like he was going to splat when he landed. Peregrine was really annoying, but he didn't deserve that, Max thought, moving to catch him.

But just before Peregrine hit the ground, two large springs sprung from the soles of his trainers. Max ducked out of the way as he landed with a bounce.

As Peregrine rebounded high into the air, Monster Max ran for the trees, but Peregrine was still holding onto the end of the elastic and Max couldn't get away. He tried to run, but the elastic rope just stretched. Peregrine followed easily on his super-springy shoes. They bounced twice around the park.

'Ha! So, I've finally got you, foul monster!' Peregrine was shouting. 'Prepare to be Portable Operating Omni Prisoned!'

Go P.O.O.P. yourself! thought Max, trying to bite through the elastic, but it was made from an extra-chewy rubber and just made a squeaky sound, like when you chew an elastic band. He looked up to see Peregrine changing the magazine on the crossbow for something big and heavy.

'Say hello to my Chain-a-Monster, mini Wookie!'

There's only one thing for it, thought Max. He opened his monster jaws as wide as he could, put the elastic rope in his mouth, then started sucking it like spaghetti. I'm going to eat that stupid machine of his, he thought. Then I'll probably chew Peregrine for a bit before I spit him out, covered in monster slime. He'll wish he ended up in the river by the time I've finished with him.

Just as he finished slurping up the

elastic rope, there was a loud twang and the sound of metal chain uncoiling, like an anchor being dropped. Before Max could stretch out his arms, they were pinned to his sides in a swirling hurricane of flying steel chain. Within half a second, he couldn't move his arms and he couldn't see. Max couldn't even roar.

'Gotcha!' Peregrine sounded quite close. 'My Chain-a-Monster works brilliantly!'

Max tried to take a deep breath and expand his chest to break the chains, but they didn't break. They did loosen around his legs, which was something, at least. They must be specially strengthened, thought Max.

'These are titanium alloy, unbreakable

for monsters!' Peregrine confirmed.

Max tried to flex his arm muscles; he bunched up hard and strained until the blood rushed in his ears and his monster eyes felt poppy. The metal dug painfully into his fur but did not break.

What was he going to do? He couldn't turn back into Max; the weight of the chains would squash him.

'Now I'm phoning the police!'

Through a tiny gap in the chain links, Max saw Peregrine take out his phone.

Just then, through another chink, Max saw a grey blur shoot across the grass and heard a familiar growl.

Mum! thought Max, very relieved she was here. Peregrine had put down his crossbow to use the phone.

'Whooo hoooo, gggrrrrrrrrrrr!' said

Max's mum.

'Aaargh!' said Peregrine. He was so
startled, he ran off, leaving his P.O.O.P.
on the ground behind him.

'Go, Max!' whispered his mother urgently. 'I'll run towards the woods, to distract him.'

This was Max's only chance. His legs were the only bit of him he might be able to get to move. Max tried jumping up and down like a pogo monster. Without the elastic rope, he might still be able to get away. He felt more chain slip and got one leg free.

With all his remaining strength, Max leapt into the air.

Normally he would have flown right over the houses, but the chains were heavy and Max was tired. Instead, he landed on some dustbins, breaking them. They smelled horrible.

Covered in slime and last night's lasagne, as well as all the chains, Max

jumped again, and again and again …
all the way to the river.

Luckily, monsters can hold their breath for hours.

Max lay underwater on the slimy bottom, hiding from Peregrine and his monster-defeating inventions until the cold grey dawn appeared.

It gave him the time to slowly and painfully unwrap the chains that were knotted about his body. It took ages, but he didn't mind, he wanted to be alone. He didn't even want his mother to find him.

In the morning light, he clambered out. Thanks to the long night underwater, he was coming down with a cold. He sneezed and, back to being plain old Max, trudged back through the lonely streets to the secret entrance at the back of his house.

When he got home, he was freezing and more tired than he had ever been in his life.

MOONLIGHT CHASE

The next day, Max did not want to get up.

He was exhausted from his long night, but he also had a lot of thoughts bouncing around in his brain like rubber balls: Peregrine almost capturing him, his mum having to save him, spending the night in cold water, how he'd have to leave his home if he and his parents got found out. The one thing he didn't feel like being ever again was a monster. That was it for monstering, and unfortunately that included protecting and doing good stuff.

His mother came into his room. She was carrying a newspaper.

'Morning, sleepy head.' She opened the curtains. Max ached all over. His arms still felt like he was wrapped up in chains.

'What time is it?'

'It's nearly 11 o'clock. But it's Saturday and you looked like you needed the sleep.'

Max watched her moving about the room through blurry eyes: she seemed a bit tired, too.

'Dad told me what happened when I got back.' She sat on the edge of the bed.

'Were you out all night, Mum?' Max

felt terrible. His mother didn't even like to stay at parties longer than 10pm.

'Don't worry, I quite enjoyed it. It's been so long … except for…'

Max's ears pricked up; something in her voice made him feel wide awake all of a sudden.

'Except for what?'

His mother looked at him and sighed, as if deciding something, and opened the paper.

THE BEAST OF BOARS HILL!!

Above the headline was a grainy CCTV shot of his mother, as a wolf, running through the long grass.

There was a long silence.

'We really do have to be careful now

– even if you are an invincible monster.'
Her eyes went sort of sparkly. 'You're
also my little boy.'

Painfully, Max sat up in bed and
forced himself to smile.

'Don't worry, Mum, I've decided I'm
never going to be a monster ever again.
I can still do good stuff,' he added, 'but
just as normal Max – like picking up
litter and making my bed. I just can't be
hairy and scary anymore.'

He thought his mum was going to be
relieved, but she frowned and shook
her head. 'No, Max, you must never
say that. You have this gift and it's a big
part of you. Always, always be yourself,
even if it has risks, even if it is very hard
sometimes.'

'But...' Max started to say, but his mum put her hand on his shoulder and looked deep into his eyes.

'Remember, we trust you. You are stronger than you think. You must push yourself to be as strong as possible. It's not just this boy, Peregrine. You were right about what you saw the night of the fire – there's other things going on. I picked up some familiar scents from the old country when I was out last night.'

Max was about to say everything was all stupid Peregrine's fault, but, before he could, his mother said, 'And you can't just be tough and scary, you also have to be smart.'

And that got him thinking again.

Max spent most of the morning in the billiard room playing Texan 8 Ball with Madame Pinky-Ponky as a way to say sorry for ruining her hat. She whipped him every game.

After his dinner (his favourite: spaghetti bolognese followed by raspberry and chocolate ripple ice cream), he watched a film about cowboys.

About half way through, his mother came into the living room. 'Well, I think I'm going to bed early,' she said and gave a giant yawn. 'Early night, I'm soooo tired. Your father is working in the library.'

'Uh, huh,' said Max. Someone had just got shot and was falling out of a window into a water trough.

'Night, Max.'

'Mmmmhm.'

After the film had finished, the house was quiet. Max wasn't a bit tired: in fact, he felt fidgety, like he had ants in his pants. He went over to the window and stared out. No sign of Peregrine. Everything was peaceful. Even the moon looked big and friendly.

He felt something brush up against his leg and looked down to see Frankenstein, who jumped up on the window ledge.

'Miaow,' he said (Frankenstein, not Max).

'You want to go out, too?' asked Max.

'Miaow, miaow,' replied Frankenstein, which Max took to mean, *You bet*.

'Well, I tell you what, we can just go for a walk, but, remember, no monstering.'

Outside the front door there was still no sign of Peregrine. I wouldn't care even if he was standing right there, thought Max.

But inside, although he would not admit it, he did feel a teeny, tiny bit nervous.

To take his mind off his nemesis, Max and Frankenstein decided to walk to the park.

It was a windy night, so the park was

empty, apart from a few ducks on the pond. Frankenstein wanted to go and have a look at them.

'Just a look,' warned Max. 'No pouncing.'

Frankenstein gave his best *Who me? I wouldn't dream of chasing a poor little duck. They are my dear friends* face, then ruined it by licking his lips.

'I think we'll go over to the swings instead,' said Max.

By now it was looking like it was going to rain: big black clouds bounced across the dark sky like grey sacks full of cold water and the chilly wind made Max shiver. Unlike his dad, he wasn't keen on clouds. It was getting too dark for Max.

'Actually, shall we just go home? Frankenstein?' He looked around but there was no sign of his cat and, with the moon covered by clouds, it really was very creepy. He squinted into the gloom and made out a shape in the grass.

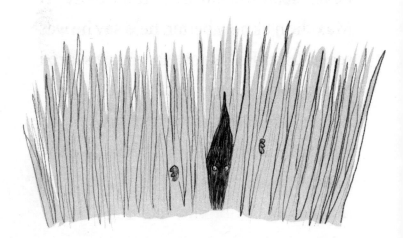

The hair on the back of his neck prickled – danger!

'Frankenstein?' he whispered into the darkness.

'Hissssss!'

'Whar!' Max gave a jump.

Frankenstein had crept up beside him and was hissing and staring in the same direction as Max, every hair standing up on his own skinny back. Max had never seen his cat like this before. If Max didn't know better, he'd say he was scared. But Frankenstein wasn't scared of anything. Except baths and salad.

So, who, or what, was the dark shape in the grass? Max peered into the gloomy night: it waited there, silent and unmoving.

Max immediately felt like burping, then remembered – no more monstering for him.

But...

Whatever it was could be dangerous and they were in a park and parks had people in – kids! If there was something dangerous out there in the long grass, they needed protecting. Suddenly all his different thoughts that day seemed to be racing into his brain at once: he remembered his mother's words – be yourself – and he thought about what his dad had said about his M.O..

That meant protecting people and doing good stuff.

And to be the best at protecting people and doing good stuff meant being both Monster Max, for strength, and Max, for having ideas.

And that meant he had a job to do!

Something was lurking out there and he had to be the one to make sure nothing bad happened, even if it was risky. Even if he was a tiny bit scared. Even if people like Peregrine didn't like it.

Max crept forward with Frankenstein at his side, moving as silently as he could through the grass.

He was now only a few yards away. Every nerve was sending small alarms through his body. In spite of the chilly evening, Max felt hot and his palms were clammy.

Not yet, he told himself, still creeping forward.

Not yet.

Now!

Max jumped at the exact moment he swallowed air and burped. Leaping high up into the air as a boy, he came down all hairy and very scary.

'Grotcha!' he growled through very big teeth, his hairy arms grabbing at where the creature was sitting.

But they grabbed thin air.

Monster Max looked around in surprise and saw the shape far away, slinking off through the trees.

Max bounded after it, but as he went faster, the dark shadow seemed to go faster too and with ease.

'Gright!' said Monster Max and with a signal to his cat, he put on extra speed.

(Frankenstein knew the signal meant not to try to keep up, but to go home, which he did.)

They ran through the park and out into open countryside. Max breathed in the cold night air as he accelerated. It felt amazing. The creature was just ahead of him, but he could not get a clear view. Sometimes it seemed as if he was gaining on it, then he was slipping back.

They came to a forest. The mysterious animal slid through the trees as easily as water flows around rocks. Max smashed through anything that got in his way. Then he jumped up high and ran along the tops of the trees, growling and roaring and laughing. The threat of rain had gone by now and the moon shone brightly.

Now this was what it was all about! He loved being a monster! He was going to capture whatever it was that was running away and make sure they knew that hanging about in his park was not acceptable. Not whilst Monster Max was out there protecting and doing good stuff!

They ran for what seemed like hours. Max felt stronger and more confident with every passing tree he climbed, each rock he smashed through or thicket of brambles he gobbled up.

They climbed steep hills, streaked along chalk paths and leaped across ravines.

Max found strength and speed he never knew he had.

As the moon dimmed and dipped and the world went from silver to grey, Max and the strange creature he could never quite see turned back towards Max's town and slowed.

With a jolt of alarm, Max realised they were heading towards his street.

The grey shape he had been following also slowed. It turned into Honeybrooke Road.

Max waited but, by now, he already knew.

Four paws became two legs and walked up the path to his house. The creature was still covered in fur but Max would have recognised that walk anywhere. Just before she went inside, she turned and looked at him with the same smile, the same sparkly brown eyes – a bit like his – that he saw every night just before he went to sleep and every morning at breakfast.

His mum.

But why had she run away? Max thought about it and it was obvious: she'd done it to show him how strong he really was. And it was true, he'd never felt so fierce or run so fast. He really was a better monster than he thought.

He was about to follow her in, when something caught Max's eye, something glinting under the trees opposite the house. Max's monster eyes peered into the dim dawn, under the shadows, and a familiar face stared out.

Peregrine!

Who had seen his mother turn from wolf to human on their very doorstep.

THE BOBBLE HAT OF FORGETTING

When Max woke, he was sure of two things. Now that Peregrine knew about his mother, he really, really needed to do something to stop him. And, secondly, he was absolutely starving. Monstering gave you a monster appetite.

'So what do I do?' said Max, through a mouthful of his sixth helping of bacon and eggs.

'Have you tried just talking to him?' his dad asked, looking up from the newspaper. His dad didn't seem that bothered about Peregrine, which Max thought was weird. 'I'm sure he's nice enough and quite normal, if you get to know him.'

'You're kidding?'

'I don't think he's your problem. Look!' He held up the newspaper. 'There's more shops and cars and things around town being smashed. It's not you. Something's up, and I think I know what it is.'

'What?'

'You told Mum you saw a little red hat and heard hammering?'

'Yup, at the dump and after the fire.'

'And saw tiny footprints in the sewer and you distinctly heard a sound like gna gna gna gna?'

'Uh huh. Could have been a dog or a rabbit.'

'And it knocked you off your feet, even when you were a monster. Doesn't sound like any rabbit I've ever heard of.'

'A Zombie Rabbit?'

'No,' said his dad, in a tone of voice that meant: don't be ridiculous.

He got up and went to the kitchen cupboard. Standing on a chair, he reached up and took hold of something hidden at the very top. It was a square package, wrapped in brown paper and tied with string.

'We were keeping this as your birthday present, but I think you could use it now.'

Max liked presents easily as much as he liked the cooked breakfasts Madame PP made, so he wasted no time in opening the satisfyingly heavy parcel. Inside there were two leather-bound books. They were old and felt expensive. *Ponder's Guide to Magical Fauna* said one in gold lettering and *Walt Stockman's Kritters of Krit* said the other.

Max would have preferred a lightsaber or a BB gun. 'I'm guessing you think the answer might be in one of these?'

'You did say you liked reading,' said his dad, smiling as if he'd just scored a goal.

Grrr, thought Max, tempted to turn himself into a monster and run through the kitchen wall. However, he could see what his dad was getting at. With a sigh, he finished his last bacon rasher, swigged the remains of his tea and picked the books up.

An hour later he found his dad in the library drawing pictures of cumulonimbus (fluffy clouds).

'It's a Grimp,' said Max, looking very pleased with himself. 'And they love smashing things up.'

'A what now?'

'Grimp.'

'You're sure you're not making it up.'

'Wish I was. So what can we do about it?'

'No, what can you do about it?' said Max's dad firmly. 'You're the monster and you've got your M.O. – to protect and do good stuff! I'd say this was right up your dark alley. But remember what your mother said yesterday?'

'Stop telling people that Madame Pinky-Ponky used to be an Olympic synchronised swimmer?'

'No, the other thing.'

Max thought about it for a bit. 'About being strong AND using my brains?'

'That's it.'

'Yes, but sometimes people are brainer than me.' Max was now thinking about Peregrine, because he basically thought about Peregrine a lot.

'I'm talking about the Grimp.'

'Well, it might be brainier than me, too. I've no idea how clever made-up creatures are.'

His mum wandered in, getting ready to go to dodgeball.

'Dad says it's up to me to do something about the Grimp, but I can't just eat it: I have to use my brain.'

'Hmm, good advice!' said Mum,

raising an eyebrow. 'As long as you promise to be careful.'

'Well, I'm glad we got that sorted,' his dad said, smiling. 'Now there's only one thing for it…'

'What?'

'You need to even things up.'

'OK, but if the books are right, I need to act fast,' said Max. 'I was reading that these creatures are fast and the longer they remain free, the stronger they get. Worse still, if one comes, more always follow and, before you know it, you'll have an army of these things running about the place smashing things with their hammers and terrifying people.'

Max stopped. Something had just occurred to him. 'And if that happens, anyone from Krit is going to be very unpopular around here.'

'Hmm.' His parents looked even more worried.

Max frowned, trying to look like he was concentrating on the Grimp problem, and not still thinking about how to get Peregrine back. Just then, something occurred to him. Something out-of-the-blue.

'What about the Bobble Hat of Forgetting?'

Both his parents looked at their feet.

'Unless you were making all that stuff up? In which case you're both terrible parents.'

'I guess it could work...' his mother said slowly, but something was clearly bothering them.

The more Max thought about it, the

better the idea seemed. No one would get eaten and the Grimp would forget to smash things up. 'So, OK, let's go and get it straight away.'

'Um … I'm not sure…' His dad looked really embarrassed now.

'What do you mean, you're not sure?'

'Well…'

'Yes, Dad?'

'You see…'

'Well, not really…'

'I've forgotten where I put it.'

Behind Max's dad, Max's mum rolled her eyes towards the ceiling.

They looked for it all day. They searched the library; they ransacked the billiard room; they opened up the ballroom and looked under the long white dust sheets;

they went into the master bedroom; the Turkish baths; into guest bedrooms 1-18 and even poked about in the cellar.

Nothing. Zip.

'Well, I've got no idea,' said his dad, as they went to the library where Madame Pinky-Ponky liked to have tea every day at 4.30 sharp.

'Hmm?' Max was distracted. Being in the cellar had given him an idea.

'We've looked everywhere.'

'There's nothing for it,' said Max. 'I'll just have to out-monster him – it, I mean. Hi, Madame PP,' he said quickly.

'Gosh, you are both very dusty. You look like you could do with some tea. I've also made scones with some of the last raspberry and crab apple jam.'

'Thanks.' Max's dad leaned forward to

grab a scone, then stopped and stared. 'Um, Max? You're looking a bit funny, you know.'

Max was goggling at the tea pot in a peculiar way. At the tea cosy, to be precise. The knitted tea cosy. With a bobble on top.

'Dad,' he murmured.

'What?' His father frowned.

'I think we found it,' said Max, slowly breaking into a grin. 'Unless I'm mistaken, that's not just a tea cosy!'

His dad looked at Max … and then at the teapot … and then back at Max. He grinned too.

'Max, you're brilliant. It's the Bobble Hat of Forgetting.' His dad said this in the way people in films said "I've found the Sword of Gryffindor" or "Look out the window, it's the Death Star".

Madame Pinky-Ponky shook her head, as if to say, Of course it is, silly, I knew all along.

Ten minutes later they were finishing up the last of the scones. The Hat lay on the table, still looking rather ordinary.

'Well, the way I see it, the problem with a Grimp isn't actually the Grimp – it's his hammer.' His dad was talking so excitedly he was spraying bits of scone across the library. 'If you can take that away and make sure he can't remember ever having it in the first place, then he'll go off and sit beside a pond in someone's garden and fish or make a little wheelbarrow and push it about. They can be lovely.'

'Like having a dog?' asked Max, who really, really wanted to have a dog but was worried about hurting Frankenstein's feelings.

'Not that nice.'

He had a few other questions, but just then the doorbell went. As usual, Max shot off to answer it.

He left the Bobble Hat on the tea tray.

Max had a nasty feeling as he walked down the hallway. He opened the door and saw a familiar pair of shiny shoes and neatly pressed nerdy trousers.

'Ha! I know it's you!' said Peregrine.

'I know it's me, too. I'm standing right here. Well, if that's all you've got to say for yourself…' Max started to close the door.

'No, I mean, I know you're hiding the monster. And I know there's a big wolf too. I've seen it go into your house. And it's your mum!'

'Good for you,' said Max, whilst thinking, Uh oh.

'Yeah, good for me.' Peregrine was looking slightly mad. He was carrying his new contraption, which had obviously being going through some improvements since Max last saw it. It still looked like a cross between a vacuum cleaner and a crossbow, but it had a new, bigger battery pack and Peregrine had stuck lightning bolts down the side. In spite of himself, Max was intrigued. He loved contraptions. He pretended to yawn, though.

'Look, I'm really tired, if you could come back tomorrow and you can bring your, um, machine.'

'My P.O.O.P..'

'That, too, if you insist.'

'Tired, are we?'

'Yes, I just said I was,' said Max.

'And I know why. Out with that monster friend of yours, being dangerous and doing bad stuff...'

'Hey, that's not true.' Max began to feel very cross. 'We're...'

He shut up, not wanting to say too much.

'...both going to prison.' Peregrine finished the sentence for him. 'That monster of yours and your mum are nothing but a menace. The sooner they're behind bars the better.'

Right, that's it! thought Max. He forgot about what his dad said about talking to Peregrine, forgot about using his brains not his monster power and, most of all, he forgot about the Bobble Hat of Forgetting.

And he burped his biggest burp ever.

10

MONSTERS V MACHINES

'Raaar raar raaaar raar raaaaar raar! Raaar raar raaaar raar raaaaar raar! Raaar raar raaaar raar raaaaar raar! Raaar raar raaaar raar raaaaar raar! Raaar raar raaaar raar raaaaar raar ... cough, deep breath ... Raaar raar raaaar raar raaaaar raar **RAAAAAAARRRRRR!'**

For a second it looked like Peregrine was going to burst into tears. One moment he was talking to Max, the next instant Max had sprouted hair and ballooned into a petrifying beast. Max the Boy felt almost sorry for him; Max the Monster thought he was an early supper.

Peregrine seemed to pull himself together. 'It was you, all the time! I knew something funny was going on!'

(Max was quite impressed. Peregrine hadn't peed in his pants, fainted, run away or done any of the things people usually did when faced with a huge bristling creature with claws and teeth like swords going *Raaar!* Spike had run away and he was twice his size and a hardened criminal, but Peregrine didn't budge.)

Peregrine pointed the P.O.O.P. machine at Max, right between his eyes. 'You're under arrest! Claws up!' The machine sprang to life: lights went on and it made a noise like a tummy rumbling.

Max wasn't going to hang around to find out what happened next. In a single bound, he leaped over Peregrine's head and scampered around the back of the house.

But not fast enough.

There was a loud zoing! and something shot past Max's head, missing him by millimetres. Whoosh, zing, doing.

He's bonkers – he's shooting fireworks at me, thought Max.

As Max got to the secret cellar

entrance, he heard Peregrine coming after him. The cellar was huge, dark and scary. Max was counting on Peregrine giving up when he saw his first spider.

(This would have been quite understandable. The spiders that lived in the dark corners underneath the house were as big as crabs and as hairy as rats, with eyes like lamplights – even Frankenstein left them alone unless he was feeling especially hungry.)

Going through the door, Max looked at all the stairs going in every direction: up, down, sideways; some wide as a car, others small, rickety and rotten. Max decided to go down, deep into the darkest and spookiest part of the house.

Taking the stone steps six at a time, he glanced back and saw Peregrine pause at the top. He squinted into the gloom before taking aim with the P.O.O.P. machine. There was a loud twang and Max felt a strong net wrap itself around his arms and legs.

He fell.

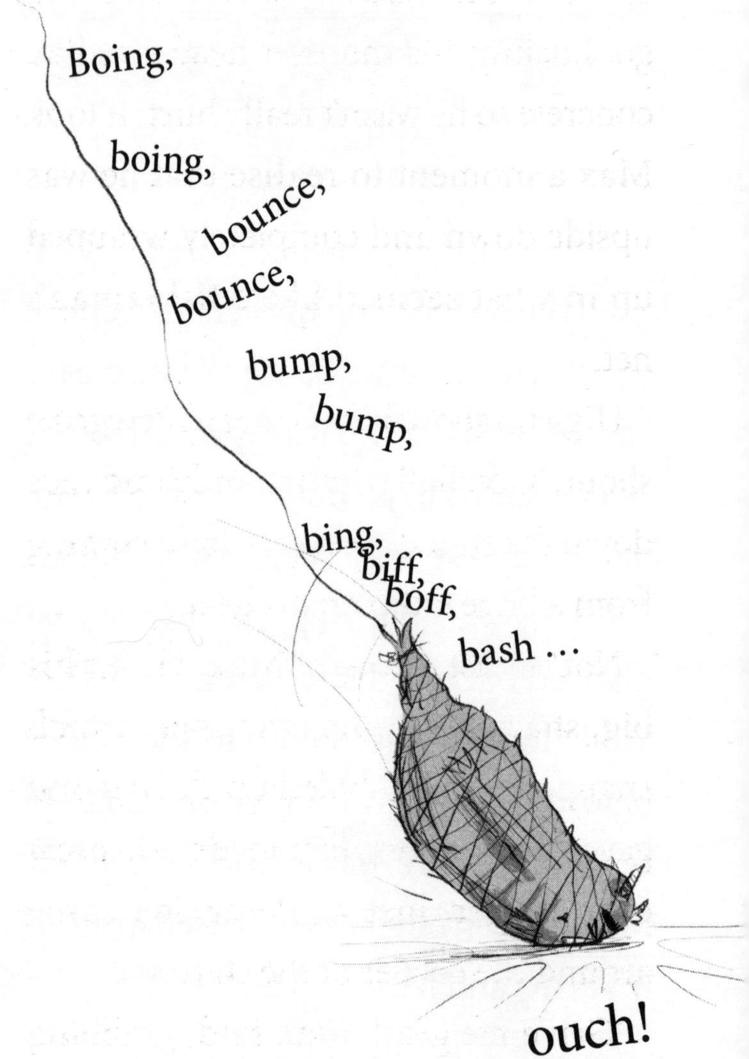

Boing,

boing,

bounce,

bounce,

bump,

bump,

bing,
biff,
boff,
bash ...

ouch!

Max fell all the way to the very bottom of the staircase, as far down as he could go. Luckily, his monster head was like concrete so he wasn't really hurt. It took Max a moment to realise that he was upside down and completely wrapped up in what seemed like a fisherman's net.

High up above him, he heard Peregrine shout, 'Gotcha!' triumphantly and race down the stairs, a beam of light coming from a huge lamp on his head.

Not so fast, thought Max. He bit his big, sharp teeth into the rope, which snapped. Max gobbled up the net and gave another burp that made him grow even bigger, just as Peregrine came around the corner of the staircase.

'Grive me grat!' Max said, grabbing

the P.O.O.P. machine from the surprised Peregrine and snapping it in half. 'Gright, now you!' he growled, preparing to spring at Peregrine.

As he took a deep breath to give his biggest roar yet, a spider web went up his nose.

Max sneezed.

Drat!

'Hello, Peregrine,' said Max. 'Oh, blimey, look what's behind you...' he said, pointing over Peregrine's shoulder. Peregrine just smiled.

'You must think I'm as stupid as you look right now.'

Max felt the chilly cellar air around his bare bottom. He'd forgotten his cape again.

He pulled his now-very-baggy pants

up as Peregrine raised one half of the broken P.O.O.P. machine. 'It's broken but I've got one shot left. Prepare to meet the Stinger!'

'Seriously, I'd turn around if I were you.' Something in Max's voice made Peregrine pause.

Max burped, just as Peregrine felt the first of eight very hairy legs start to climb onto his shoulder.

Now, Max had been exploring the cellar since he was six and knew it better than anyone alive. He knew, for example, that in the gloom just above their heads was a long metal chain used for taking heavy sacks of coal from the cellar that ran all the way to the top of the roof. It was old and very rusty, but thick enough to carry his monster weight.

Just as Peregrine screamed, 'Help, I hate spiders more than anything, even broccoli!' Max did a double somersault and grabbed the chain.

'Brye, brye!' he growled, and started climbing as fast as he could.

There was a loud **ZINNNGG!** noise and a rather unhappy-looking spider sailed past Max, its hairy legs and body fizzing with electricity. That must have been the Stinger.

Max felt a tug of the chain and his monster eyes, with their extra special night vision, saw Peregrine climbing up the rope after him. What was worse, Peregrine seemed to be catching up. Two mechanical arms had grown out of his back and were doing the climbing for him. Max was almost impressed.

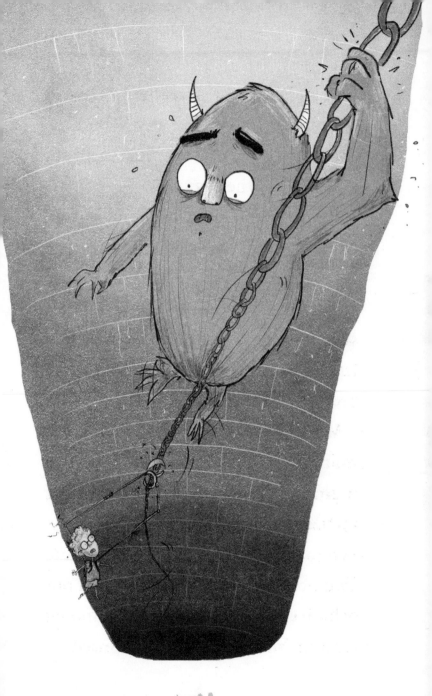

'Ha! Foul Monster, you hadn't counted on that! Face it, your strength is no match for my amazing inventions!'

With a whirring noise like a helicopter taking off, the mechanical arms shot forward, climbing the chain faster than Max ever could. He remembered what his mother said about using his brains, but it was difficult coming up with a super plan when climbing a rusty metal chain in the dark.

Seeing a staircase through the gloom on his left, Max leaped towards it, just as a cold, mechanical arm grabbed him. Landing badly on the crumbling stone, pinned by one of the metal arms, he kicked up a cloud of dust.

Max sneezed again.

'I've got you now,' said Peregrine, his

mechanical arm pulling Max the Boy closer.

Max, in his stretched underpants, dangled in mid-air in front of his nemesis. This was highly embarrassing. But Peregrine looked quite tired: the mechanical arm was slipping on the metal chain and he also needed both his real hands to hold on. He looked puzzled.

'Some of the things you can do are amazing.'

'Does that mean you're not going to hand me over to the police?'

'I … er…' Peregrine, for once, didn't seem so sure of himself. 'I know all your secrets, and now I've got you just where I want…'

But he didn't get to finish his sentence.

'Gna gna gna gna gnaaa!' said something that wasn't Max or Peregrine (or even Frankenstein) and a small shape with a red hat shot out of a hole in the wall. 'Gna gna gna gna gnaaa!'

It whizzed off towards another hole on the other side of the cellar. Before it disappeared, the small creature stopped and turned towards Max.

'Bbbbblllaaaaa!' It blew a raspberry and made a very rude sign.

'What was that?' asked Peregrine.

'It's a Grimp!' said Max, pleased to know something Peregrine didn't.

Ha, not so clever after all, thought Max.

But, to spoil it, Max did something stupid – he burped. Seeing the Grimp made his protect and do good stuff brain take over.

Several things happened very quickly:

- Peregrine's mechanical arms snapped: they were made for climbing and holding small boys, not big monsters.
- The chain snapped: it was rustier than Max had remembered and also didn't like all this extra weight of boys, monsters and mechanical arms.
- Max, who was now right at the top of the long chain, started to fall. At the last moment he grabbed hold of a ledge with his incredibly strong monster claws.
- Peregrine also fell and would have continued all the way to the bottom, if Max hadn't grabbed him with his other monster arm.

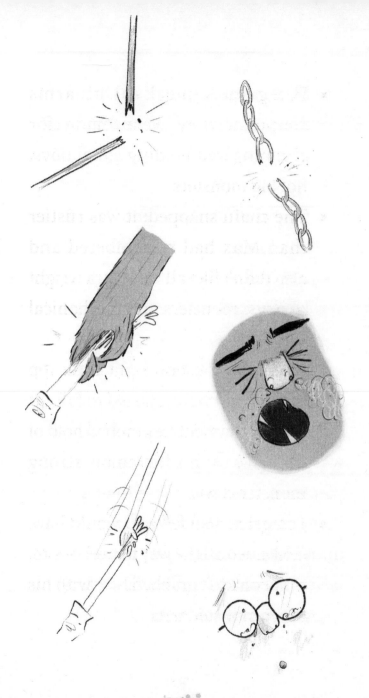

- Max sneezed again (it was incredibly dusty down there, someone really ought to clean up once in a while).
- Now he was no longer a monster, the weight of holding on to Peregrine was too much … almost.
- … but Max held on.
- He looked into Peregrine's eyes and saw just a boy, about his own age, looking back. A boy who was frightened.

To protect and do good stuff, that was Max's M.O.: it didn't matter who you were, Max was there to help. And Peregrine was like lots of people – he didn't like monsters just because he'd never met one as cool and nice as Max.

'Don't worry,' said Max. 'I won't let go.'

11

PEREGRINE AND MONSTER OR
MONSTER AND PEREGRINE

'So you're friends now?'

Max's dad was busy with his cloud maps, but he took an interest when Max came into the library with Peregrine to borrow a large sheet of paper, some colouring pens and a ruler.

'Yup,' replied Max. 'All I had to do was save him from certain death. Now I just need to do the same for the other fifty-million-nine-hundred-thousand-nine-hundred-and-ninety people in Britain and hairy monsters will be more popular than Christmas.'

'Very pleased to meet you, Mr Max's Dad,' said Peregrine.

'Ah, good manners. Why can't you have good manners, Max?' asked Max's dad, smiling.

'Hey!'

'Well, it's true.'

'Where's Mum?'

'It's Monday: base jumping.'

'Oh, OK.'

'Anyway, you and Peregrine deciding to stop fighting is not a moment too soon. She says you'll have to sort the Grimp out on your own. I suppose that's why you're in the library?'

'You suppose quite right.'

'Except he won't be alone,' Peregrine said, staring at the rows of books. 'I'm here to help. Gosh, what a lot of books – this place is amazing. It's so big. How's it done?'

'Reverse Cloud Technology,' said Max's dad, looking smug.

'Oh, here we go,' said Max.

'Really?' Peregrine looked very interested.

'Yes – it works like this: clouds look huge on the outside but on the inside there's not much to them. I just created a reverse field around the house with very powerful magnets, and all this space appeared. Amazing.'

'Amazing!' Peregrine agreed.

'Don't listen to him; we just had an extension built.'

'Oh,' Peregrine sounded disappointed.

'Right, Dad, I need all the books we've got on these Grimps. We've got some planning to do.'

An hour later, Madame Pinky-Ponky came into the library carrying a tea tray with chocolate cake, scones, jam, cream and, well, tea.

'Oooh, you've got a little friend?' she said, peering at Peregrine then at the large table in the centre of the library. It was covered in books, sketches of machines (by Peregrine) and doodles of hairy bottoms (by Max).

'Meet Peregrine,' said Max to Madame Pinky-Ponky. 'Peregrine, meet Madame Pinky-Ponky.'

'Hello, young man.'

'Bonjour, Madame Pinky-Ponky,' he said.

'Ooh, he's got lovely manners. Why don't you have such lovely manners?'

'Oh, good grief.'

'Anyway, what are you doing, making a mess?' Madame PP perched the tray next to a large pile of screwed-up paper.

'We're trying to work out how to get rid of this Grimp,' said Max. 'We've got the Bobble Hat of Forgetting, now we just need a plan to catch him. But he doesn't hang about. We don't want to hurt him, either.'

'So you'll still be needing my tea cosy, I suppose?'

'Interesting,' murmured Peregrine, who picked up the Bobble Hat of Forgetting for about the tenth time, looking at it very hard. 'It seems like a woolly hat, but my fingers are tingling.'

'That's the magic.'

'How does it work?'

Max's dad smiled. 'Well, you just need to get the Bobble Hat on the Grimp's head and he'll instantly forget everything, even his hammer, as long as he is wearing it. But he's been here so long now, he'll be getting stronger and stronger. The main thing is not to let him back into town. This time he won't just break a few windows. Remember, they get smarter, too. He must not get to town!'

STAKEOUT

An hour later, they had a plan. An incredible plan! The best plan since Max had planned to put his bath on wheels and have an inside-out submarine (it worked but the bath water got cold half way to the park).

Actually, it was quite simple.

They (Peregrine, mainly) had researched all the stories in the newspaper where things had been smashed (not by Max), then drawn a map. This showed that the Grimp always followed the same route into town (via the cellar in Honeybrooke Rd, then along the river Thames). They marked the spot just before the old city walls in red biro. 'We'll catch him here!' cried Peregrine confidently.

Max was incredibly excited. He couldn't wait…

…but six hours later…

Max was really, really bored.

'This Grimp's never going to come. Maybe he just stayed in the cellar.'

Peregrine, who was reading a book, didn't even bother to look up. 'He'll come and when he does, we'll be ready.'

Max thought about using the Bobble

Hat of Forgetting on Peregrine and going home to watch TV, then remembered he was meant to be protecting and doing good stuff, not just having fun.

'What's that book you're reading?'

'You wouldn't like it. It doesn't have any pictures in it,' replied Peregrine.

'Oh, ha ha – well, we've got a library with over 1000 books,' said Max.

'We've got four, and one of those is a colouring-in book.'

'Seriously?'

'My dad says you don't need books now everyone's got the internet and my mum doesn't like them because they get dusty … my parents are not so bad, I guess,' said Peregrine quickly, 'they just prefer watching TV.'

'Then, how come you're so brainy?'

'The library,' said Peregrine, going back to his book in a way that suggested he didn't want to talk about it anymore. Max decided it was best to change the subject.

'You sure that thing will work?' Max looked at the repaired P.O.O.P. machine.

'Of course I'm sure, and I've even added some new features. Look.' Peregrine pointed the pointy bit at Frankenstein and pulled the trigger. Instantly a cage flew out of the machine and trapped Max's cat.

Frankenstein gave a startled miaow and Max said, 'Cor!' again.

Peregrine looked pleased with himself. 'This Grimp of yours won't be able to resist stopping for the trap we've made and when he does we'll be ready with my P.O.O.P..'

'I'll never get tired of hearing you say that,' said Max, but he had to admit the booby trap was good. Max looked at the row of bottles on the city wall: big ones, small ones, blue ones, green ones, some empty, some full of fizzy liquid – Max would have liked to smash them himself.

There was no way the Grimp would be able to pass by without stopping to break the bottles with his hammer.

But when?

'I'm still bor–' Max started to say, but just then his hair started to stand on end and his monster ears pricked up.

Peregrine, who was folding the cage back into his P.O.O.P. machine, looked up.

'What is it?'

'I dunno,' said Max. 'I can hear something that sounds like a Grimp, but it's not quite right. It sounds too far away or…'

'Or what?' Peregrine was looking hard at Max. Even Frankenstein had stopped pacing about; his tatty ears flicking this way and that.

'It's…' Max strained his ears as hard as he could.

He could hear a very faint 'gna gna gna gna gna' from far off but somehow just below.

'He's under our feet!' he exclaimed. 'The Grimp must be going through the rabbit holes! That's why he was in the tunnel in the cellar. Now, that is clever!'

'Curses, our plan hasn't worked.'

Peregrine looked thoughtful. 'We need a new plan fast,' he said to Max, 'or the Grimp will reach town and start destroying everything!'

'I know just what we need,' said Max with a wicked grin.

And he burped.

Monster Max had never dug before, but with his strong arms and claws it was easy. Also, the Grimp was smashing through the narrow rabbit holes, to make them wider, and making a lot of noise, so he wasn't hard to follow.

Max had dug down, found the hole and now was racing after the pesky creature. Peregrine was following.

Bang, bang, bang, **DONK!**

'What's happening?' Peregrine's glasses were covered in mud and he was exhausted.

'It's gropped,' said Max, stopping himself. 'Wall, just dere,' he said, pointing a claw through the gloom.

There was a sudden flare of incredibly bright light, as Peregrine turned the headlights of the P.O.O.P. machine on.

'Gnaa, gnaaa, gnaaaaaaaa!' squealed the Grimp, who was covered in mud as well, and trying to bang a hole in a huge underground wall that marked the edge of the city.

'Gaaa, gright lights, turn dem groff,' said Monster Max.

'He's just a titchy little man,' said Peregrine. 'Can't see what all the fuss is about.' Anything he was about to add was cut short by the huge ball of mud the Grimp threw in Peregrine's face.

'Greally?' said Monster Max.

'Right,' said Peregrine, wiping huge clumps of mud out of his eyes and ears, 'that does it. Quick, before he starts to tunnel up! Remember what your dad said: he must not reach town.' He took aim with the P.O.O.P. and fired.

ZANG!

The cage flew out and trapped the Grimp against the underground wall.

'Gna gna gna!' the little man squeaked in rage.

'Quick, grab the bobble hat!' cried Peregrine, taking it from his anorak pocket. 'Put it on him.'

Bang, bang, **BANG!**

But they were not quick enough: there

was a massive explosion of twisted metal and the cage flew apart. The Grimp whizzed past them, digging through the roof of the tunnel to get outside.

'Gret gre grincers, gret gre grincers!' Monster Max jumped up and down like a big hairy beach ball.

'The what?'

Max made mechanical arm grabbing actions with his claws.

'Oh, the pincers – good idea!' From out of his anorak sprung the grabbers Peregrine had used for climbing up the iron chain. They shot forward to catch the Grimp, who was nearly at the surface.

At the same time, Monster Max leaped up and grabbed hold of the Grimp's tiny but very strong feet. Its head was nearly poking through into fresh air.

Bang, bang, bang: the little hammer hammered Max's head.

'Grouch, grouch, grouch,' said Monster Max. 'Grurry up!' He glared at Peregrine.

'I am hurrying up,' said Peregrine. 'It's not easy working these things underground. Sorry!' he called, as the pincers pinched Max's bottom.

With the banging on his head and Peregrine attacking him from behind, Max wasn't sure he could hold on much longer.

Just then, there was a funny noise. **WHOOOM**, ping.

'Grot gros grat?'

'I've lost power. I never had enough time to recharge before we went out this evening!' shouted Peregrine, fiddling with the useless controls of the grabber.

'Gro no!' said Max.

The wriggling Grimp was going to be free in any second. He could feel his claws slipping. He had a horrible thought, imagining things all over town being smashed and his family getting the blame.

'You can't hold on much longer,' said Peregrine, who could see Max's arms beginning to shake. But Max knew that if he let go, the Grimp would escape.

The Grimp was incredibly strong. It was like trying to hold onto a miniature but very powerful rocket. Max's claws were getting tired and the Grimp began to wriggle free… The town would be in ruins…

Miaow.

Everyone had quite forgotten about Frankenstein, but just then he chose to stroll down the tunnel. Instantly, the Grimp stopped hitting Max.

'Eeek, Bad Pussycat!' the little man cried, and tried to hide behind Max.

'He's scared of your cat,' said Peregrine.

'Quick! Gris could be our only grance!' shouted Max. The Grimp seemed to be frozen to the spot with fear.

For the moment.

Peregrine threw the Bobble Hat to Max. Max caught it, whipped off the Grimp's red pointy cap and replaced it with the Bobble Hat of Forgetting.

The small man froze and his eyes went swirly as he slid down the wall.

Peregrine stepped forward and took the hammer out of his stiff fingers. 'I'll be having that,' he said. 'And you really ought to turn back into Max the Boy. Don't want to scare him.'

'How do dat?'

'Here's how,' said Peregrine, bringing out some pepper. 'I had a feeling we might need it.'

'Granks, you grink of everything,' said Max.

'Someone has to.'

'Atishoo! Yuk! I don't suppose you've got a hanky? Ah, thanks.'

'Don't mention it.'

'Ooh, I like his little coat, and his cute little red boots,' said Max, going over. 'Can we keep him?'

'No, we can't,' said Peregrine. 'Look, he's coming round.'

'Where am I?' said the Grimp in a voice like a squeaky toy.

'You're on your way home,' said Peregrine firmly.

'Really?'

'Yes, really,' said Peregrine.

He fished about in one of his pockets and brought out what looked like a squashed sponge. Peregrine gave it a squeeze and it immediately inflated into a square box with squidgy sides.

'I didn't have much time, but I managed to design this before we came out. It's a travelling box with padded walls for extra comfort, a light and aircon. I call it Peregrine's Pod.'

'A PeePee!' Max simply couldn't help

himself. There was a click as the front opened and a warm orange light went on.

'If you'd like to step this way,' said Peregrine, ignoring Max. 'I think I've got the size right for you. The pet courier company will be here to pick you up in...' He checked his watch. 'Four minutes and twenty seconds.'

'Unbelievable,' said Max, who was both impressed and horrified that anyone his age could be that organised.

'OK,' said the Grimp, stepping through the little open door. 'It is nice and cosy in here, I must say.'

'That's just why you like it,' said Max, whipping the Bobble Hat off the Grimp's head, now it had done its job. Madame Pinky-Ponky would be needing it back for teatimes. 'And we'll be sure to come and visit when you get back to Krit!' Max had decided it was probably best they didn't keep him. Frankenstein would get jealous.

'Sure, just don't bring any cats. Hate 'em.'

'Well done,' said Max to his new friend as they climbed out of the tunnel. 'That was pretty good fun, wasn't it?'

Peregrine turned around and almost smiled. 'Well, I suppose we make a good team,' he said. 'Peregrine the Genius Inventor and his hairy sidekick, Max the Monster. I can see it in all the best newspapers.'

'I think you mean Max the Monster and his trusty assistant, Master Peregrine.'

'Doesn't work for me,' said Peregrine.

'Well, the other way around is just wrong.'

'No, it's not.'

And they argued about it as they walked home for supper together.

END OF BOOK ONE

EPILOGUE

A thousand miles away, a lone wolf padded through the forest. His black fur was darker than the night and made him almost invisible in the murky woods. His eyes glowed red in the darkness. Something made him stop as he came to a track. At the edge of the path a box rested on some moss. A Grimp was sitting on a stone outside the strange-looking container, polishing his hammer. The box was definitely not from Krit but, much more importantly, the small creature's scent reminded Fanghorn of someone he knew long ago. Someone he had never forgotten. He padded up to the Grimp as silent as oil moving across water.

'Eek!' the Grimp squeaked in fear as soon as he noticed the large wolf looming over him.

'So where have you been little man?' hissed the wolf. 'Tell me everything.'

Find out more about Max at:

www.monstermax.co.uk

Win prizes!

Read exclusive stories

Build your own Peregrine machines

and be first to get the latest news on Monster Max and his new adventures.

Uncover the magic and the mysteries of Krit. Here are just a few of the strange (and very rare!) creatures you might meet if you trekked to the top of the mountain.

Kritters Of Krit

By Walter J Stockman, the Third 1897
Residing at The Maryland Home
for Muddled Gentlefolk

LYCHANTHROPE

These shapeshifters patrol Krit to deter unwanted visitors. Around half the time, they take human form. When they change, they can be anything: bears, eagles ... and even hairy monsters who own unsavoury pet cats.

The largest group – and the cleverest – are the wolves. These are the Kings and Queens of Krit.

They are separated into Clans by eye colour: the shy silver are the best hunters; greys are the wisest and most gentle. Then there are the brooding, dangerous reds ... if you upset them, they will find you. Oh, yes.

M

Shy Silver

Brooding reds

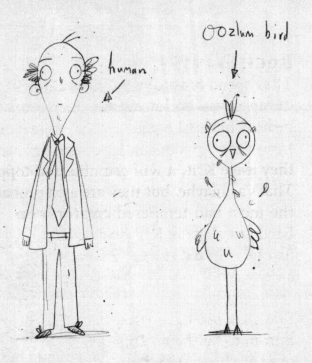

human

Oozlum bird

OOZLUM BIRD

In human form, they are bumbling, slightly forgetful humans, who often become teachers in subjects no one does any more – like Astronomy or Bagpiping. As birds, they are totally rubbish: they literally never look where they are going. Every Oozlum bird that ever lived has, at one point in their lives, flown headfirst into a cow's bottom. It's a rite of, ahem, passage.

ROCK GIANT

They spend most of their lives alone in the damp caves hollowed out deep into the bedrock of Krit. Legend says they were created from the very roots of the mountain and, if they leave Krit, it will crumble and topple. That's as maybe, but they are also probably the most bad-tempered creatures on Earth, let alone in Krit, so it might just be worth it if they did go away.

Rock Giants have been known to hit themselves over the head with tree stumps if there is no one else to pick a fight with. They smell awful, too. Seriously, if you're really desperate for a tall friend, buy a giraffe.

Rock giant

ICE WITCH

Definitely not the cuddly sort of granny witch, who makes cures for coughs and tummy ache. Ice Witches are a fusion of cold calculation and permafrost. Screech Witch is another name for them: you get the picture. Steeped in powerful magic, even Reds are respectful to them.

Iu Witch

So these are just a very few of the marvellous, magical animals of Krit. Once upon a time they were only found in this tiny kingdom, hidden in the clouds but they're on the move … and coming to a story near you …

MONSTER MAX

Totaleee amazing and very cool!
'To protect and do good stuff' - no job too small.

PS Peregrine looks like a dorky hamster.

Max